T0150387

KING LEOPOLD'S SOLILOQUY

MARK TWAIN

INTRODUCTION BY HUNT HAWKINS

UNO Press
Manufactured in the United States of America
All rights reserved
ISBN: 9781608011186

Book and cover design: Alex Dimeff

UNO PRESS
unopress.org

KING LEOPOLD'S SOLILOQUY

MARK TWAIN

INTRODUCTION BY HUNT HAWKINS

UNO PRESS

INTRODUCTION
Hunt Hawkins

Mark Twain wrote *King Leopold's Soliloquy* at the
request of Edmund Dene Morel, head of the British Congo Reform Association, who visited him
in New York on October 17, 1904. Finished in late
February 1905, it was published on September 28
as a pamphlet by the American Congo Reform
Association, which brought out a second edition
on January 1, 1906. Twain donated all proceeds to
them.

This satire attacks King Leopold II of Belgium,
who at the Berlin Conference of 1885 got control of
the Congo as his personal territory, not as a Belgian
colony. In 1892 Leopold instituted a brutal system
of forced labor to collect ivory and wild rubber.
During his rule, at least two million Congolese
were killed, a precursor as Hannah Arendt argues
of the genocides to come. Some estimates run as
high as the ten million given by Twain. Many were
mutilated since Leopold stipulated that a severed
hand be returned for every cartridge expended
by his *Force Publique*. At Twain's suggestion, the
pamphlet contained photos taken by missionaries
of mutilated Africans.

The form of *King Leopold's Soliloquy* matches Twain's "The Czar's Soliloquy" published in the March 1905 *North American Review*. Both are dramatic monologues in which a villain gives an outrageously inadequate defense of himself. In *King Leopold's Soliloquy* the King reads frequently from articles attacking him. Twain thus documents Leopold's crimes at the same time the King sputters feebly against his attackers.

Even though Twain himself never visited the Congo or had any personal connection with it, his motives for writing *King Leopold's Soliloquy* had deep roots. He had a life-long interest in issues of race and slavery, evidenced most notably in his masterpieces *Huckleberry Finn* (1885) and *Pudd'nhead Wilson* (1894). More immediately, he had become immersed in issues of imperialism as a result of his around-the-world lecture tour of 1895-96, which he undertook to pay off creditors following his bankruptcy. This tour took him to the British colonies of Fiji, Australia, New Zealand, Ceylon, India, and South Africa. Twain found he could not support the idea of whites having a cultural superiority that justified imperialism. In *Following the Equator*, Twain's book about his trip, he wrote, "There are many humorous things in the world, among them the white man's notion that he is less savage than the other savages." Imperialism also conflicted with Twain's belief in the democratic principles articulated by Washington, Jefferson, and Lincoln.

When he finally returned to the United States in 1900, Twain announced, "I am an anti-imperialist." He became a Vice-President of the Anti-Imperialist League joining his friend William Dean Howells and such diverse notables as Grover

Cleveland, Andrew Carnegie, and Samuel Gompers. The League opposed U. S. annexation of the Philippines following the Spanish-American War of 1898, an annexation Rudyard Kipling encouraged in his poem "The White Man's Burden." In letters, interviews, speeches, and articles, Twain protested the British in the Boer War in South Africa, supported the Chinese in the Boxer Rebellion, opposed Russian seizure of Port Arthur and Manchuria, and attacked the United States during its 1899-1902 war to take over the Philippines amid Filipino resistance under the leadership of Emilio Aguinaldo after Spain had ceded its colony to the U. S. Twain's published anti-imperialist articles include the short "A Salutation Speech from the Nineteenth Century to the Twentieth" in the *New York Herald* on December 30, 1900 and three longer ones in the *North American Review*: his best and most famous "To the Person Sitting in Darkness" in February 1901, "To My Missionary Critics" in April 1901, and "A Defense of General Funston" in May 1902.

E. D. Morel undoubtedly approached Twain about the Congo in 1904 owing to his fame both as an author and an anti-imperialist. Twain concluded that Leopold was "a bloody monster whose mate is not findable in human history anywhere." For the next year-and-a-half Twain involved himself heavily in Congo reform. He became First Vice-President of the American Congo Reform Association, wrote two shorter pieces that remained unpublished, gave a lengthy newspaper interview, mentioned reform in several speeches, and made three trips to Washington to talk with President Theodore Roosevelt and high officials at the State Department. Leopold's ambassador

Baron Moncheur set up a lobbying group in the United States to counteract reform, producing an anonymous forty-seven-page pamphlet, *An Answer to Mark Twain*.

Unfortunately, during his involvement, Twain made the mistake of assuming the U. S. had ratified the Berlin Treaty and therefore had a legal interest in the Congo. In *King Leopold's Soliloquy* he had the King say, "America and thirteen great European states wept in sympathy with me [. . .] their representatives met in convention in Berlin and made me Head Foreman and Superintendent of the Congo State." When the State Department informed him that President Cleveland had in fact withheld the Berlin Treaty from Senate ratification, Twain concluded it was useless to agitate in America. He resigned from the Congo Reform Association on February 10, 1906.

Twain had other reasons for resigning. At age 70 he had neither the strength nor desire to keep up with the demands of the movement. He had recurrent bronchitis and angina, and had never fully recovered from the death of his wife Olivia in 1904. He wrote Dr. Thomas Barbour, a reform leader, "My instincts & interests are merely literary, they rise no higher [. . .] I am not a bee, I am a lightning-bug." Twain's feelings mirror those of Joseph Conrad, who contributed a broadside to the British Congo Reform Association but in 1903 refused further aid by writing, "I would help [. . .] but it is not in me. I am only a wretched novelist inventing wretched stories and not even up to that miserable game."

At a more abstract level, Twain was succumbing to the pessimism that filled his final years. His growing belief in determinism, similar to that of the Naturalists and expressed in late essays such as "What Is Man?" (1906), meant villains could not be held responsible for their actions and reformers couldn't change the public. The public, in fact, was too cowardly ever to stand up to a tyrant. This pessimism even infects Twain's reformist pamphlet. He has King Leopold say of humanity, "A curious race, certainly! It finds fault with me and my occupations, and forgets that neither of us [Leopold and the Czar] could exist for an hour without its sanction. It is our confederate and all-powerful protector." When reformers tried to re-engage Twain, he wrote, "The woes of the wronged & the unfortunate poison my life & make it so undesirable that pretty often I wish I were 90 instead of 70."

Twain isolated himself so completely from the Congo Reform Association that he seems never to have learned that it was ultimately successful. On December 11, 1906, referring to enormous public pressure, President Roosevelt wrote the British Foreign Secretary that he was ready to move against Leopold, now citing U. S. participation in the Declaration of Brussels in 1890 as legal basis. In 1908 Belgium took control of the Congo from Leopold. Thus Twain's brave if wavering humanitarian efforts finally bore fruit even though he himself never knew it.

"It Is I"

Leopold II is the absolute
Master of the whole of the
internal and external activity
of the Independent State of the
Congo. The organization of
justice, the army, the industrial
and commercial regimes are established freely by himself.
He would say, and with greater accuracy than did Louis
XIV, "The State, it is I." *Prof. F. Cattier, Brussels University.*
Let us repeat after so many others what has become a
platitude, the success of the African work is the work of a
sole directing will, without being hampered by the hesi-
tation of timorous politicians, carried out under his sole
responsibility—intelligent,
thoughtful, conscious of the
perils and the advantages,
discounting with an admirable
prescience the great results
of a near future. *M. Alfred
Poskine in "Bilans Congolais."*

"A memorial for the perpetuation of
my name."—*Page 25*

KING LEOPOLD'S SOLILOQUY

[Throws down pamphlets which he has been reading. Excitedly combs his flowing spread of whiskers with his fingers; pounds the table with his fists; lets off brisk volleys of unsanctified language at brief intervals, repentantly drooping his head, between volleys, and kissing the Louis XI crucifix banging from his neck, accompanying the kisses with mumbled apologies; presently rises, flushed and perspiring, and walks the floor, gesticulating]

—!!——!! If I had them by the throat! *[Hastily kisses the crucifix, and mumbles]* In these twenty years I have spent millions to keep the press of the two hemispheres quiet, and still these leaks keep on occurring. I have spent other millions on religion and art, and what do I get for it? Nothing. Not a compliment. These generosities are studiedly ignored, in print. In print I get nothing but slanders—and slanders again—and still slanders, and slanders on top of slanders! Grant them true, what of it? They are slanders all the same, when uttered against a king.

Miscreants—they are telling *everything!* Oh, everything: how I went pilgriming among the Powers in tears, with my mouth full of Bible and my pelt oozing piety at every pore, and implored them to place the vast and rich and populous Congo Free State in trust in my hands as their agent, so that I might root out slavery and stop the slave raids, and lift up those twenty-five millions of gentle and harmless blacks out of darkness into light, the light of our blessed Redeemer, the light that streams from his holy Word, the light that makes glorious our noble civilization—lift them up and dry their tears and fill their bruised hearts with joy and gratitude—lift them up and make them comprehend that they were no longer outcasts and forsaken, but our very brothers in Christ; how America and thirteen great European states wept in sympathy with me, and were persuaded; how their representatives met in convention in Berlin and made me Head Foreman and Superintendent of the Congo State, and drafted out my powers and limitations, carefully guarding the persons and liberties and properties of the natives against hurt and harm; forbidding whisky traffic and gun traffic; providing courts of justice; making commerce free and fetterless to the merchants and traders of all nations, and welcoming and safeguarding all missionaries of all creeds and denominations. They have told how I planned and prepared my establishment and selected my horde of officials—"pals" and "pimps" of mine, "unspeakable Belgians" every one—and hoisted my flag, and "took in" a President of the United States, and got him to be the first to recognize it and salute it. Oh, well, let them—blackguard me if they like; it is a deep satisfaction to me to remember that I was a shade too smart for that nation that thinks itself so smart. Yes, I certainly did bunco a Yankee—as those people phrase it. Pirate flag? Let them call it so—perhaps it is. All the same, *they were the first to salute it.*

These meddlesome American missionaries! these frank British consuls! these blabbing Belgian-born traitor officials!—those tiresome parrots are always talking, always telling. They have told how for twenty years I have ruled the Congo State not as a trustee of the Powers, an agent, a subordinate, a foreman, but as a sovereign—sovereign over a fruitful domain four times as large as the German Empire—sovereign absolute, irresponsible, above all law; trampling the Berlin-made

"They were the first to salute it"

Congo charter under foot; barring out all foreign traders but myself; restricting commerce to myself, through concessionaires who are my creatures and confederates; seizing and holding the State as my personal property, the whole of its vast revenues as my private "swag"—mine, solely mine—claiming and holding its millions of people as my private property, my serfs, my slaves; their labor mine, with or without wage; the food they raise not their property but mine; the rubber, the ivory and all the other riches of the land mine—mine solely—and gathered for me by the men, the women and the little children under compulsion of lash and bullet, fire, starvation, mutilation and the halter.

These pests!—it is as I say, they have kept back nothing! They have revealed these and yet other details which shame should have kept them silent about, since they were exposures of a king, a sacred personage and immune from reproach, by right of his selection and appointment to his great office by God himself; a king whose acts cannot be criticized without blasphemy, since God has observed them from the beginning and has manifested no dissatisfaction with them, nor shown disapproval of them, nor hampered nor interrupted them in any way. By this sign I recognize his approval of what I have done; his cordial and glad approval, I am sure I may say.

Blest, crowned, beatified with this great reward, this golden reward, this unspeakably precious reward, why should I care for men's cursings and revilings of me? *[With a sudden outburst of feeling]* May they roast a million eons in—

[Catches his breath and effusively kisses the crucifix; sorrowfully murmurs, "I shall get myself damned yet, with these indiscretions of speech."]

Yes, they go on telling everything, these chatterers! They tell how I levy incredibly burdensome taxes upon the natives—taxes which are a pure theft; taxes which they must satisfy by gathering rubber under hard and constantly harder conditions, and by raising and furnishing food supplies gratis—and it all comes out that, when they fall short of their tasks through hunger, sickness, despair, and ceaseless and exhausting labor without rest, and forsake their homes and flee to the woods to escape punishment, my black soldiers, drawn from unfriendly tribes, and instigated and directed by my Belgians, hunt them down and butcher them and burn their villages—reserving some of the girls. They tell it all: how I am wiping a nation of friendless creatures out of existence by every form of murder, for my private pocket's sake, and how every shilling I get costs a rape, a mutilation or a life. But they never say, although they know it, that I have labored in the cause of religion at the same time and all the time, and have sent missionaries there (of a "convenient stripe," as they phrase it), to teach them the error of their ways and bring them to Him who is all mercy and love, and who is the sleepless guardian and friend of all who suffer. They tell only what is against me, they will not tell what is in my favor.

They tell how England required of me a Commission of Inquiry into Congo atrocities, and how, to quiet that meddling country, with its disagreeable Congo Reform Association, made up of earls and bishops and John Morleys and university grandees and other dudes, more interested in other people's business than in their own, I appointed it. Did it stop their mouths? No, they merely pointed out that it was a commission composed wholly of my "Congo butchers," "the very men whose acts were to be inquired into." They said it was equivalent to appointing a commission of wolves to inquire into depredations committed upon a sheepfold. *Nothing* can satisfy a cursed Englishman!*

---

* This visit had a more fortunate result than was anticipated. One member of the Commission was a leading Congo official, another an official of the government in Belgium, the third a Swiss jurist. It was feared that the work of the Commission would not be more genuine than that of innumerable so-called "investigations" by local officials. But it appears that the Commission was met by a very avalanche of awful testimony. One who was present at a public hearing writes: "Men of stone would be moved by the stories that are being unfolded as the Commission probes into the awful history of rubber collection." It is evident the commissioners were moved. Of their report and its bearing upon the international issue presented by the conceded conditions in the Congo State, something is said on a supplementary

And were the fault-finders frank with my private character? They could not be more so if I were a plebeian, a peasant, a mechanic. They remind the world that from the earliest days my house has been chapel and brothel combined, and both industries working full time; that I practiced cruelties upon my queen and my daughters, and supplemented them with daily shame and humiliations; that, when my queen lay in the happy refuge of her coffin, and a daughter implored me on her knees to let her look for the last time upon her mother's face, I refused; and that, three years ago, not being satisfied with the stolen spoils of a whole alien nation, I robbed my own child of her property and appeared by proxy in court, a spectacle to the civilized world, to defend the act and complete the crime. It is as I have said: they are unfair, unjust; they will resurrect and give new currency to such things as those, or to any other things that count against me, but they will not mention any act of mine that is in my favor. I have spent more money on art than any other monarch of my time, and they know it. Do they speak of it, do they tell about it? No, they do not. They prefer to work up what they call "ghastly statistics" into offensive kindergarten object lessons, whose purpose is to make sentimental people shudder, and prejudice them against me. They remark that "if the innocent blood shed in the Congo State by King Leopold were put in buckets and the buckets placed side by side, the line would stretch 2000 miles; if the skeletons of his ten millions of starved and butchered dead could rise up

page of this pamphlet. Certain reforms were ordered by the Commission of Inquiry in the one section visited, but the latest word is that after its departure conditions were soon worse than before its coming. —M. T.

and march in single file, it would take them seven months and four days to pass a given point; if compacted together in a body, they would occupy more ground than St. Louis covers, World's Fair and all; if they should all clap their bony hands at once, the grisly crash would be heard at a distance of—" Damnation, it makes me tired! And they do similar miracles with the money I have distilled from that blood and put into my pocket. They pile it into Egyptian pyramids; they carpet Saharas with it; they spread it across the sky, and the shadow it casts makes twilight in the earth. And the tears I have caused, the hearts I have broken—oh, nothing can persuade them to let *them* alone!

[Meditative pause] Well...no matter, I *did* beat the Yankees, anyway! there's comfort in that. *[Reads with mocking smile, the "President's Order of Recognition of April 22, 1884"]*

> "...the government of the United States announces its sympathy with and approval of the humane and benevolent purposes of (my Congo scheme), and will order the officers of the United States, both on land and sea, to recognize its flag as the flag of a friendly government."

Possibly the Yankees would like to take that back, now, but they will find that my agents are not over there in America for nothing. But there is no danger; neither nations nor governments can afford to confess a blunder.

[With a contented smile, begins to read from "Report by Rev. W. M. Morrison, American missionary in the Congo Free State"]

> "I furnish herewith some of the many atrocious incidents which have come under my own personal observation; they reveal the *organized*

"They tell only what is against
me."—*Page 11*

system of plunder and outrage which has been perpetrated and is now being carried on in that unfortunate country by King Leopold of Belgium. I say King Leopold, because he and he *alone* is now responsible, since he is the *absolute sovereign. He styles himself such.* When our government in 1884 laid the foundation of the Congo Free State, by recognizing its flag, little did it know that this concern, parading under the guise of philanthropy—was really King Leopold of Belgium, one of the shrewdest, most heartless and most conscienceless rulers that ever sat on a throne. This is apart from his known corrupt morals, which have made his name and his family a byword in two continents. Our government would most certainly not have recognized that flag had it known that it was really King Leopold individually who was asking for recognition; had it known that it was setting up in the heart of Africa an *absolute monarchy,* had it known that, having put down African slavery in our own country at great cost of blood and money, it was *establishing a worse form of slavery right in Africa."*

[*With evil joy*] Yes, I certainly was a shade too clever for the Yankees. It hurts; it gravels them. They can't get over it! Puts a shame upon them in another way, too, and a graver way; for they never can rid their records of the reproachful fact that their vain Republic, self-appointed Champion and Promoter of the Liberties of the World, is the only democracy in history that has lent its power and influence to the establishing of an *absolute monarchy!*

[*Contemplating, with an unfriendly eye, a stately pile of pamphlets*] Blister the meddlesome missionaries! They write tons of these things. They seem to be always around, always spying, always eye-witnessing the happenings; and everything they see they commit to paper. They are always prowling from place to place; the natives consider them their only friends; they go to them with their sorrows; they show them their scars and their wounds, inflicted by my soldier police; they hold up the stumps of their arms and lament because their hands have been chopped off, as punishment

"They go to them with their sorrows"

for not bringing in enough rubber, and as proof to be laid before my officers that the required punishment was well and truly carried out. One of these missionaries saw eighty-one of these hands drying over a fire for transmission to my officials—and of course he must go and set it down and print it. They travel and travel, they spy and spy! And nothing is too trivial for them to print.

[Takes up a pamphlet. Reads a passage from Report of a "Journey made in July, August and September, 1903, by Rev. A. E. Scrivener, a British missionary"]

"....Soon we began talking, and without any encouragement on my part the natives began the tales I had become so accustomed to. They were living in peace and quietness when the white men came in from the lake with all sorts of requests to do this and that, and they thought it meant slavery. So they attempted to keep the white men out of their country but without avail. The rifles were too much for them. So they submitted and made up their minds to do the best they could under the altered circumstances. First came the command to build houses for the

soldiers, and this was done without a murmur.
Then they had to feed the soldiers and all the men
and women—hangers on—who accompanied
them. Then they were told to bring in rubber.
This was quite a new thing for them to do. There
was rubber in the forest several days away from
their home, but that it was worth anything was
news to them. A small reward was offered and
a rush was made for the rubber. "What strange
white men, to give us cloth and beads for the
sap of a wild vine." They rejoiced in what they
thought their good fortune. But soon the reward
was reduced until at last they were told to bring
in the rubber for nothing. To this they tried to
demur; but to their great surprise several were
shot by the soldiers, and the rest were told, with
many curses and blows, to go at once or more
would be killed. Terrified, they began to prepare
their food for the fortnight's absence from the village which the collection of rubber entailed. The
soldiers discovered them sitting about. "What,
not gone yet?" Bang! bang! bang! and down fell
one and another, dead, in the midst of wives
and companions. There is a terrible wail and
an attempt made to prepare the dead for burial,
but this is not allowed. All must go at once to
the forest. Without food? Yes, without food. And
off the poor wretches had to go without even
their tinderboxes to make fires. Many died in the
forests of hunger and exposure, and still more
from the rifles of the ferocious soldiers in charge
of the post. In spite of all their efforts the amount
fell off and more and more were killed. I was
shown around the place, and the sites of former
big chiefs' settlements were pointed out. A careful estimate made the population of, say, seven
years ago, to be two thousand people in and
about the post, within a radius of, say, a quarter
of a mile. All told, they would not muster two
hundred now, and there is so much sadness and

"Some bones which they had seen"

gloom about them that they are fast decreasing.

"We stayed there all day on Monday and had many talks with the people. On the Sunday some of the boys had told me of some bones which they had seen, so on the Monday I asked to be shown these bones. Lying about on the grass, within a few yards of the house I was occupying, were numbers of human skulls, bones, in some cases complete skeletons. I counted thirty-six skulls, and saw many sets of bones from which the skulls were missing. I called one of the men and asked the meaning of it. "When the rubber palaver began," said he, "the soldiers shot so many we grew tired of burying, and very often we were not allowed to bury; and so just dragged the bodies out into the grass and left them. There are hundreds all around if you would like to see them." But I had seen more than enough, and was sickened by the stories that came from men and women alike of the awful time they had passed through. The Bulgarian atrocities might be considered as mildness itself when compared with what was done here. How the people submitted I don't know, and even now I wonder as I think of their patience. That some of them managed to run away is some cause for thankfulness. I stayed there two days and the one thing that impressed itself upon me was the collection of rubber. I saw long files of men come in, as at Bongo, with their little baskets under their arms; saw them paid their milk tin full of salt, and the two yards of calico flung to the headmen; saw their trembling timidity, and in fact a great deal that all went to prove the state of terrorism that exists and the virtual slavery in which the people are held."

That is their way; they spy and spy, and run into print with every foolish trifle. And that British consul, Mr. Casement, is just like them. He gets hold of a *diary which had been kept by one of my government officers*, and, although it is a private diary and intended for no eye but its owner's, Mr. Casement is so lacking in delicacy and refinement as to print passages from it. *[Reads a passage from the diary]*

"Each time the corporal goes out to get rubber, cartridges are given him. He must bring back all not used, and for every one used he must bring back a right hand. M. P. told me that sometimes they shot a cartridge at an animal in hunting; they then cut off a hand from a living man. As to the extent to which this is carried on, he informed me that in six months the State on the Mambogo River had used six thousand cartridges, which means that six thousand people arc killed or mutilated. It means more than six thousand…for the people have told me repeatedly that the soldiers kill the children with the butt of their guns."

When the subtle consul thinks silence will be more effective than words, he employs it. Here he leaves it to be recognized that a thousand killings and mutilations a month is a large output for so small a region as the Mambogo River concession, silently indicating the dimensions of it by accompanying his report with a map of the prodigious Congo State, in which there is not room for so small an object as that river. That silence is intended to say, "If it is a thousand a month in this little corner, imagine the output of the whole vast State!" A gentleman would not descend to these furtivenesses.

Now as to the mutilations. You can't head off a Congo critic and make him stay headed-off; he dodges, and straightway comes back at you from another direction. They are full of slippery arts. When the mutilations (severing hands, unsexing men, etc.) began to stir Europe, we hit upon the idea of excusing them with a retort which we judged would knock them dizzy on that subject for good and all, and leave them nothing more to say; to wit, we boldly laid the custom on the natives, and said we did not invent it, but only followed it. Did it knock them dizzy? did it shut their mouths? Not for an hour. They dodged, and came straight back at us with the remark that "if a Christian king can perceive a saving moral difference between inventing bloody barbarities, and *imitating them from savages,* for charity's sake let him get what comfort he can out of his confession!"

It is most amazing, the way that that consul acts—that spy, that busy-body. *[Takes up pamphlet "Treatment of Women and Children in the Congo State; what Mr. Casement Saw in 1903"] Hardly two years ago! Intruding* that date upon the public was a piece of cold malice. It is intended to weaken the force of my press syndicate's assurances to

FOOT AND HAND OF CHILD DISMEMBERED BY SOLDIERS,
BROUGHT TO MISSIONARIES BY DAZED FATHER. FROM
PHOTOGRAPH TAKEN AT BARINGA, CONGO STATE, MAY
15, 1904. SEE MEMORIAL TO CONGRESS JANUARY, 1905.

"Imagine the output of the whole vast
state!"—*Page 18*

the public that my severities in the Congo *ceased,* and ceased utterly, *years and years ago.* This man is fond of trifles—revels in them, gloats over them, pets them, fondles them, sets them all down. One doesn't need to drowse through his monotonous report to see that; the mere sub-headings of its chapters prove it. *[Reads]*

> "Two hundred and forty persons, *men, women and children,* compelled to supply government with *one ton* of carefully prepared foodstuffs *per week,* receiving in remuneration, all told, the princely sum of 15s 10d.!"

Very well, it was liberal. It was not much short of a penny a week for each nigger. It suits this consul to belittle it, yet he knows very well that I could have had both the food and the labor for nothing. I can prove it by a thousand instances. *[Reads]*

> "Expedition against a village behindhand in its (compulsory) supplies; result, slaughter of sixteen persons; among them three women and a boy of five years. Ten carried off, to be prisoners till ransomed; among them a child, who died during the march."

But he is careful not to explain that we are *obliged* to resort to ransom to collect debts, where the people have nothing to pay with. Families that escape to the woods sell some of their members into slavery and thus provide the ransom. He knows that I would stop this if I could find a less objectionable way to collect their debts... Mm—here is some more of the consul's delicacy! He reports a conversation he had with some natives:

Q. How do you know it was the *white* men themselves who ordered these cruel things to be done to you? These things must have been done without the white man's knowledge by the black soldiers.

A. These white men told their soldiers: "You only kill *women*; you cannot kill men. You must prove that you kill men." So then the soldiers when they killed us (here he stopped and hesitated and then pointing to ... he said:) then they...and took them to the white men, who said: "It is true, you have killed *men*."

Q. You say this is true? Were many of you so treated after being shot?

All *[shouting out]*: Nkoto! Nkoto! (Very many! Very many!)

There was no doubt that these people were not inventing. Their vehemence, their flashing eyes, their excitement, were not simulated.

Of course the critic had to divulge that; he has no self-respect. All his kind reproach me, although they know quite well that I took no pleasure in punishing the men in that particular way, but only did it as a warning to other delinquents. Ordinary punishments are no good with ignorant savages; they make no impression. *[Reads more sub-heads]*

"Devastated region; population reduced from forty thousand to eight thousand."

He does not take the trouble to say how it happened. He is fertile in concealments. He hopes his readers and his Congo reformers, of the Lord-Aberdeen-Norbury-John-Morley-Sir-Gilbert-Parker stripe, will think they were all killed. They were not. The great majority of them escaped. They fled to the bush with their families because of the rubber raids, and it was there they died of hunger. Could we help that?

One of my sorrowing critics observes: "Other Christian rulers tax their people, but furnish schools, courts of law, roads, light, water and protection to life and limb in return; King Leopold taxes his stolen nation, but provides *nothing in return but hunger, terror, grief, shame, captivity, mutilation and massacre.*" That is their style! I furnish "nothing"! I send the gospel to the survivors; these censure-mongers know it, but they would rather have their tongues cut out than mention it. I have several times required my raiders to give the dying an opportunity to kiss the sacred emblem; and if they obeyed me I have without doubt been the humble means of saving many souls. None of my traducers have had the fairness to mention this; but let it pass; there is One who has not overlooked it, and that is my solace, that is my consolation.

[Puts down the Report, takes up a pamphlet, glances along the middle of it.]

On Dress Parade

This is where the "death-trap" comes in. Meddlesome missionary spying around—Rev. W. II. Sheppard. Talks with a black raider of mine after a raid; cozens him into giving away some particulars:

"I demanded 30 slaves from this side of the stream and 30 from the other side; 2 points of ivory, 2,500 balls of rubber, 13 goats, 10 fowls and 6 dogs, some corn chumy, etc," [the raider remarks.]

'How did the fight come up?' I asked.

'I sent for all their chiefs, sub-chiefs, men and women, to come on a certain day, saying that I was going to finish all the palaver. When they entered these small gates (the walls being made of fences brought from other villages, the high native ones) I demanded all my pay or I would kill them; so they refused to pay me, and I ordered the fence to be closed so they couldn't run away; then we killed them here inside the fence. The panels of the fence fell down and some escaped.'

'How many did you kill?' I asked.

'We killed plenty, will you see some of them?'

That was just what I wanted.

He said: 'I think we have killed between eighty and ninety, and those in the other villages I don't know, I did not go out but sent my people.'

He and I walked out on the plain just near the camp. There were three dead bodies with the flesh carved off from the waist down.

'Why are they carved so, only leaving the bones?' I asked.

'My people ate them,' he answered promptly. He then explained, 'The men who have young children do not eat people, but all the rest ate them.'

On the left was a big man, shot in the back and without a head. (All corpses were nude.)

'Where is the man's head?' I asked.

'Oh, they made a bowl of the forehead to rub up tobacco and diamba in.'

We continued to walk and examine until late in the afternoon, and counted forty-one bodies. The rest had been eaten up by the people.

On returning to the camp, we crossed a young woman, shot in the back of the head, one hand was cut away. I asked why, and Mulunba N'Cusa explained that they always cut off the right hand to give to the State on their return.

'Can you not show me some of the hands?' I asked.

So he conducted us to a framework of sticks, under which was burning a slow fire, and there they were, the right hands—I counted eighty-one in all.

There were not less than sixty women (Bena Pianga) prisoners. I saw them.

We say that we have as fully as possible investigated the whole outrage, and find it was a plan previously made to get all the stuff possible and to catch and kill the poor people in the death-trap.

Another detail, as we see!—cannibalism. They report cases of it with a most offensive frequency. My traducers do not forget to remark that, inasmuch as I am absolute and with a word can prevent in the Congo anything I choose to prevent, then whatsoever is done there by my permission is my act, my *personal* act; that *I* do it; that the hand of my agent is as truly *my* hand as if it were attached to my own arm; and so they picture me in my robes of state, with my crown on my head, munching human flesh, saying grace, mumbling thanks to Him from whom all good things come. Dear, dear, when the soft-hearts get

MULUNBA CHIEF OF CANNIBAL TRIBE NEAR LUEBO, CONGO
STATE FIGURE REPRODUCED FROM PHOTOGRAPH

"Mulunba N'Cusa explained."—*Page 24*

hold of a thing like that missionary's contribution they completely lose their tranquility over it. They speak profanely and reproach Heaven for allowing such a fiend to live. Meaning me. They think it irregular. They go shuddering around, brooding over the reduction of that Congo population from 25, 000,000 to 15,000,000 in the twenty years of my administration; then they burst out and call me "the King with Ten Million Murders on his Soul." They call me a "record." The most of them do not stop with charging merely the 10,000,000 against me. No, they reflect that but for me the population, by natural increase, would now be 30,000,000, so they charge another 5,000,000 against me and make my total death-harvest 15,000,000. They remark that the man who killed the goose that laid the golden egg was responsible for the eggs she would subsequently have laid if she had been let alone. Oh, yes, they call me a "record." They remark that twice in a generation, in India, the Great Famine destroys 2,000,000 out of a population of 320,000,000, and the whole world holds up its hands in pity and horror; then they fall to wondering where the world would find room for its emotions if I had a chance to trade places with the Great Famine for twenty years! The idea fires their fancy, and they go on and imagine the Famine coming in state at the end of the twenty years and prostrating itself before me, saying: "Teach me, Lord, I perceive that I am but an apprentice." And next they imagine Death coming, with his scythe and hourglass, and begging me to marry his daughter and reorganize his plant and run the business. For the whole world, you see! By this time their diseased minds arc under full steam, and they get down their books and expand their labors, with me for text. They hunt through all biography for my match, working Attila, Torquemada, Genghis Khan, Ivan the Terrible, and the rest of that crowd for all they are worth, and evilly exulting when they cannot find it. Then they examine the historical earthquakes and cyclones and blizzards and cataclysms and volcanic eruptions: verdict, none of them "in it" with me. At last they do really hit it (as they think), and they close their labors with conceding—reluctantly—that I have *one* match in history, but only one—the *Flood*. This is intemperate.

But they are always that, when they think of me. They can no more keep quiet when my name is mentioned than can a glass of water control its feelings with a seidlitz powder in its bowels. The bizarre things they can imagine, with me for an inspiration! One Englishman offers to give me the odds of three to one and bet me anything I like, up to 20,000 guineas, that for 2,000,000 years I am going to be the most conspicuous foreigner in hell. The man is so beside himself with anger that he does not perceive that the idea is foolish. Foolish and unbusinesslike: you see, there could be no winner; both of us would be losers, on account of the loss of interest on the stakes; at four or five per cent compounded, this would amount to—I do not know how much, exactly, but, by the time the term was up and the bet payable, a person could buy hell itself with the accumulation.

Another madman wants to construct a memorial for the perpetuation of my name, out of my fifteen thousand skulls and skeletons, and is full of vindictive enthusiasm over his strange project. He has it all ciphered out and drawn to scale. Out of the skulls he will build a combined monument and mausoleum to me which shall exactly duplicate the Great Pyramid of Cheops, whose base covers thirteen acres, and whose apex is 451 feet above ground. He desires to stuff me and stand me up in the sky on that apex, robed and crowned, with my "pirate flag" in one hand and a butcher knife and pendant handcuffs in the other. He will build the pyramid in the center of a depopulated tract, a brooding solitude covered with weeds and the moldering ruins of burned villages, where the spirits of the starved and murdered dead will voice their laments forever in the whispers of the wandering winds. Radiating from the pyramid, like the spokes of a wheel, there are to be forty grand avenues of approach, each thirty-five miles long, and each fenced on both sides by skull-less skeletons standing a yard and a half apart and festooned together in line by short chains stretching from wrist to wrist and attached to tried and true old handcuffs stamped with my private trade-mark, a crucifix and butcher-knife crossed, with motto, "By this sign we prosper"; each osseous fence to consist of 200,000 skeletons on a side, which is 400,000 to each avenue. It is remarked with satisfaction that it aggregates three or four thousand miles (single-ranked) of skeletons—15,000,000 all told—and would stretch across America from New York to San Francisco. It is remarked further, in the hopeful tone of a railroad company forecasting showy extensions of its mileage, that my output is 500,000 corpses a year when my plant is running full time, and that therefore if I am spared ten years longer there will be fresh skulls enough to add 175 feet to the pyramid, making it by a long way the loftiest architectural construction on the earth, and fresh skeletons

"My yearly income from the Congo is
millions of guineas."—*Page 30*

enough to continue the transcontinental file (on piles) a thousand miles into the Pacific. The cost of gathering the materials from my "widely scattered and innumerable private graveyards," and transporting them, and building the monument and the radiating grand avenues, is duly ciphered out, running into an aggregate of millions of guineas, and then—why then, (—!! —!!) this idiot asks me *to furnish the money! [Sudden and effusive application of the crucifix]* He reminds me that my yearly income from the Congo is millions of guineas, and that only 5,000,000 would be required for his enterprise. Every day wild attempts are made upon my purse; they do not affect me, they cost me not a thought. But *this one*—this one troubles me, makes me nervous; for there is no telling what an unhinged creature like this may think of next...*If he should think of Carnegie*—but I must banish that thought out of my mind! it worries my days; it troubles my sleep. That way lies madness. *[After a pause]* There is no other way—I have got to buy Carnegie.

[Harassed and muttering, walks the floor a while, then takes to the Consul's chapter-headings again. Reads]

> Government starved a woman's children to death and killed her sons.
> Butchery of women and children.
> *The native has been converted into a being without ambition because without hope.*
> Women chained by the neck by rubber sentries.
> Women refuse to bear children because, with a baby to carry, they cannot well run away and hide from the soldiers.
> Statement of a child: "I, my mother, my grandmother and my sister, we ran away into the

bush. A great number of our people were killed by the soldiers....After that they saw a little bit of my mother's head, and the soldiers ran quickly to where we were and caught my grandmother, my mother, my sister and another little one younger than us. Each wanted my mother for a wife, and argued about it, so they finally decided to kill her. They shot her through the stomach with a gun and she fell, and when I saw that I cried very much because they killed my grand-mother and mother and I was left alone. I saw it all done!"

"Women chained by the neck"

It has a sort of pitiful sound, although they are only blacks. It carries me back and back into the past, to when my children were little, and would fly—to the bush, so to speak—when they saw me coming....[Resumes the reading of chapter-headings of the Consul's report]

They put a knife through a child's stomach.

They cut off the hands and brought them to C. D. (white officer) and spread them out in a row for him to see. They left them lying there, because the white man had seen them, so they did not need to take them to P.

Captured children left in the bush to die, by the soldiers.

Friends came to ransom a captured girl; but sentry refused, saying the white man wanted her because she was young.

Extract from a native girl's testimony: "On our way the soldiers saw a little child, and when they went to kill it the child laughed, so the soldier took the butt of his gun and struck the child with it and then cut off its head. One day

*"Somehow—I wish it
had not laughed"*

they killed my half-sister and cut off her head, hands and feet, because she had bangles on. Then they caught another sister, and sold her to the W. W. people and now she is a slave there."

The little child laughed! *[A long pause. Musing]* That innocent creature. Somehow—I wish it had not laughed.
[Reads]

Mutilated children.
Government encouragement of inter-tribal slave-traffic. The monstrous fines levied upon villages tardy in their supplies of foodstuffs compel the natives to sell their fellows—and children—to other tribes in order to meet the fine.
A father and mother forced to sell their boy.
Widow forced to sell her little girl.

[Irritated] Hang the monotonous grumbler, what would he have me do! Let a widow off merely because she is a widow? He knows quite well that there is nothing much left, now, *but* widows. I have nothing against widows, as a class, but business is business, and I've got to live, haven't I, even if it does cause inconvenience to somebody here and there?*[Reads]*

Men intimidated by the torture of their wives and daughters. (To make the men furnish rubber and supplies and so get their captured women released from chains and detention.) The sentry explained to me that he caught the women and brought them in (chained together neck to neck) by direction of his employer.

An agent explained that he was forced to catch women in preference to men, as then the men brought in supplies quicker; but he did not explain how the children deprived of their parents obtained their own food supplies.

A file of 15 (captured) women.

Allowing women and children to die of starvation in prison.

[Musing] Death from *hunger.* A lingering, long misery that must be. Days and days, and still days and days, the forces of the body failing, dribbling away, little by little—yes, it must be the hardest death of all. And to see food carried by, every day, and you can have none of it! Of course the little children cry for it, and that wrings the mother's heart....

[A sigh] Ah, well, it cannot be helped; circumstances make this discipline necessary. *[Reads]*

The crucifying of sixty women!

How stupid, how tactless! Christendom's goose flesh will rise with horror at the news. "Profanation of the sacred emblem!" That is what Christendom will shout. Yes, Christendom will buzz. It can hear me charged with half a million murders a year for twenty years and keep its composure, but to profane the Symbol is quite another matter. It will regard this as serious. It will wake up and want to look into my record. Buzz? Indeed it will; I seem to hear the distant hum already....It was wrong to crucify the women, clearly wrong, manifestly wrong, I can see it now, myself, and am sorry it happened, sincerely sorry. I believe it would have answered just as well to skin them.... *[With a sigh]* But none of us thought of that; one cannot think of everything; and after all it is but human to err.

It will make a stir, no doubt, these crucifixions. Persons will begin to ask once more, as now and then in times past, how I can hope to win and keep the respect of the human race if I continue to give up my life to murder and pillage. *[Scornfully]* When have they heard me say I wanted the respect of the human race? Do they confuse me with the common herd? Do they forget that I am a king? What king has valued the respect of the human race? I mean deep down in his private heart. If they would reflect, they would know that it is impossible that a king should value the respect of the human race. He stands upon an eminence and looks out over the world and sees multitudes of meek human things worshiping the persons, and submitting to the oppressions and exactions, of a dozen human things who are in no way better or finer than themselves—made on just their own pattern, in fact, and out of the same quality of mud. When it *talks*, it is a race of whales; but a king knows it for a race of tadpoles. Its history gives it away. If men were really *men*, how could a Czar be possible? And how could I be possible? But we *are* possible; we are quite safe; and with God's help we shall continue the business at the old stand. It will be found that the race will put up with us, in its docile immemorial way. It may pull a wry face now and then, and make large talk, but it will stay on its knees all the same.

"*Made on just their own pattern*"

Making large talk is one of its specialties. It works itself up, and froths at the mouth, and just

when you think it is going to throw a brick—it
heaves a poem! Lord, what a race it is!

A CZAR - 1905

A pasteboard autocrat; a despot out of date;
    A fading planet in the glare of day;
    A flickering candle in the bright sun's ray,
Burnt to the socket; fruit left too late,
    High on a blighted bough, ripe till it's rotten.

    By God forsaken and by time forgotten,
Watching the crumbling edges of his lands,
    A spineless god to whom dumb millions pray,
    From Finland in the West to far Cathay,
Lord of a frost-bound continent he stands,
    Her seeming ruin his dim mind appalls,
And in the frozen stupor of his sleep
    He hears dull thunders, pealing as she falls,
And mighty fragments dropping in the deep.*

It is fine, one is obliged to concede it; it is a
great picture, and impressive. The mongrel han-
dles his pen well. Still, with opportunity, I would
cruci—flay him..."A spineless god." It is the Czar
to a dot—a god, and spineless; a royal inverte-
brate, poor lad; softhearted and out of place. "A
spineless god *to whom dumb millions pray.*"

Remorselessly correct; concise, too, compact—
the soul and spirit of the human race compressed
into half a sentence. On their knees—140,000,000.
On their knees to a little tin deity. Massed together,
they would stretch away, and away, and away,
across the plains, fading and dimming and failing
in a measureless perspective—why, even the tele-
scope's vision could not reach to the final frontier
of that continental spread of human servility. Now

*   B. H. Nadal, in *New York Times.*

why should a king value the respect of the human race? It is quite unreasonable to expect it. A curious race, certainly! It finds fault with me and with my occupations, and forgets that neither of us could exist an hour without its sanction. It is our confederate and all-powerful protector. It is our bulwark, our friend, our fortress. For this it has our gratitude, our deep and honest gratitude—but not our respect. Let it snivel and fret and grumble if it likes; that is all right; we do not mind that.

[Turns over leaves of a scrapbook, pausing now and then to read a clipping and make a comment]

The poets—how they do hunt that poor Czar! French, Germans, English, Americans—they all have a bark at him. The finest and capablest of the pack, and the fiercest, are Swilburne (English, I think), and a pair of Americans, Thomas Bailey Eldridge and Colonel Richard Waterson Gilder, of the sentimental periodical called *Century Magazine* and *Louisville Courier-Journal.* They certainly have uttered some very strong yelps. I can't seem to find them—I must have mislaid them...If a poet's bite were as terrible as his bark, why dear me—but it isn't. A wise king minds neither of them; but the poet doesn't know it. It's a case of little dog and lightning express. When the Czar goes thundering by, the poet skips out and rages alongside for a little distance, then returns to his kennel wagging his head with satisfaction, and thinks he has inflicted a memorable scare, whereas nothing has really happened—the Czar didn't know he was around. They never bark at me; I wonder why that is. I suppose my Corruption-Department buys them. That must be it, for certainly I ought to inspire a bark or two; I'm rather choice material, I should say. Why—here *is* a yelp at me. *[Mumbling a poem]*

...What gives thee holy right to murder hope
    And water ignorance with human blood?

From what high universe-dividing power Draw'st
thou thy wondrous, ripe brutality?

O horrible ... Thou God who seest these things
Help us to blot this terror from the earth.

...No, I see it is *To the Czar*[*] after all. But there are
those who would say it fits me—and rather snugly,
too. "Ripe brutality." They would say the Czar's
isn't ripe yet, but that mine is; and not merely ripe
but rotten. Nothing could keep them from saying
that; they would think it smart. "This terror." Let
the Czar keep that name; I am supplied. This long
time I have been "the monster;" that was their fa-
vorite—the monster of crime. But now I have a new
one. They have found a fossil Dinosaur fifty-seven
feet long and sixteen feet high, and set it up in the
museum in New York and labeled it "Leopold II."
But it is no matter, one does not look for manners
in a republic. Um...that reminds me; I have never
been caricatured. Could it be that the corsairs of the
pencil could not find an offensive symbol that was
big enough and ugly enough to do my reputation
justice? *[After reflection]* There is no other way—I
will buy the Dinosaur. And suppress it. *[Rests himself with some more chapter-headings. Reads]*

More mutilation of children. (Hands cut off.)
Testimony of American Missionaries. Evidence of
British Missionaries.

It is all the same old thing—tedious repeti-
tions and duplications of shop-worn episodes;

---

[*]   Louise Morgan Sill, in *Harper's Weekly*.

mutilations, murders, massacres, and so on, and so on, till one gets drowsy over it. Mr. Morel intrudes at this point, and contributes a comment which he could just as well have kept to himself— and throws in some italics, of course; these people can never get along without italics:

> It is one heartrending story of human misery from beginning to end, and *it is all recent.*

Meaning 1904 and 1905. I do not see how a person can act so. This Morel is a king's subject, and reverence for monarchy should have restrained him from reflecting upon me with that exposure. This Morel is a reformer; a Congo reformer. That sizes *him* up. He publishes a sheet in Liverpool called *The West African Mail,* which is supported by the voluntary contributions of the sap-headed and the soft-hearted; and every week it steams and reeks and festers with up-to-date "Congo atrocities" of the sort detailed in this pile of pamphlets here. I will suppress it. I suppressed a Congo atrocity book there, after it was actually in print; it should not be difficult for me to suppress a newspaper.

[Studies some photographs of mutilated Negroes, throws them down. Sighs] The Kodak has been a sore calamity to us. The most powerful enemy indeed. In the early years we had no trouble in getting the press to "expose" the tales of the mutilations as slanders, lies, inventions of busy-body American missionaries and exasperated foreigners who found the "open door" of the Berlin-Congo charter closed against them when they innocently went out there to trade; and by the press's help we got the Christian nations everywhere to turn an irritated and unbelieving ear to those tales and say

hard things about the tellers of them. Yes, all things went harmoniously and pleasantly in those good days, and I was looked up to as the benefactor of a downtrodden and friendless people. Then all of a sudden came the crash! That is to say, the incorruptible *Kodak*—and all the harmony went to hell! The only witness I have encountered in my long experience that I couldn't bribe. Every Yankee missionary and every inter-rupted trader sent home and got one; and now—oh, well, the pictures get sneaked around everywhere, in spite of all we can do to ferret them out and suppress them. Ten thousand pulpits and ten thousand presses arc saying the good word for me all the time and placidly and convincingly denying the mutilations. Then that trivial little Kodak, that a child can carry in its pocket,

"The only witness I couldn't bribe"

gets up, uttering never a word, and knocks them dumb!....What is this fragment? *[Reads]*

But enough of trying to tally off his crimes! His list is interminable, we should never get to the end of it. His awful shadow lies across his Congo Free State, and under it an unoffending nation of 15,000,000 is withering away and swiftly succumbing of their miseries. It is a land of graves; it is *The* Land of Graves; it is the Congo Free Graveyard. It is a majestic thought: that is, this ghastliest episode in all human history is the work of *one man alone;* one solitary man; just a single individual—Leopold, King of the Belgians. He is personally and solely responsible for all the myriad crimes that have blackened the history of the Congo State. He is *sole* master

FROM PHOTOGRAPHS, CONGO STATE

"The pictures get sneaked around everywhere"
—*Page 39*

there; he is absolute. He could have prevented the crimes by his mere command; he could stop them today with a word. He withholds the word. For his pocket's sake.

It seems strange to see a king destroying a nation and laying waste a country for mere sordid money's sake, and solely and only for that. Lust of conquest is royal; kings have always exercised that stately vice; we are used to it, by old habit we condone it, perceiving a certain dignity in it; but *lust of money—lust of shillings—lust of nickels—lust of dirty coin*, not for the nation's enrichment but for *the king's alone*—this is new. It distinctly revolts us, we cannot seem to reconcile ourselves to it, we resent it, we despise it, we say it is shabby, un-kingly, out of character. Being democrats we ought to jeer and jest, we ought to rejoice to see the purple dragged in the dirt, but—well, account for it as we may, we don't. We see this awful king, this pitiless and blood-drenched king, this money-crazy king towering toward the sky in a world-solitude of sordid crime, unfellowed and apart from the human race, sole butcher for personal gain findable in all his caste, ancient or modern, pagan or Christian, proper and legitimate target for the scorn of the lowest and the highest, and the execrations of all who hold in cold esteem the oppressor and the coward; and—well, it is a mystery, but *we do not wish to look*; for he is a king, and it hurts us, it troubles us, by ancient and inherited instinct it shames us to see a king degraded to this aspect, and we shrink from hearing the particulars of how it happened. *We shudder* and *turn away* when we come upon them in print.

Why, certainly—THAT IS MY PROTECTION. And you will continue to do it. I know the human race.

FROM PHOTOGRAPH, IKOKO, CONGO STATE

"To THEM is must appear very awful and
mysterious"—Joseph Conrad

AN ORIGINAL
M I S T A K E

This work of "civilization" is
an enormous and continual
butchery. All the facts we
brought forward in this cham-
ber were denied at first most
energetically; but later, little
by little, they were proved by documents and by official
texts. The practice of cutting off hands is said to be contrary
to instructions; but you are content to say that indulgence
must be shown and that this bad habit must be correct-
ed "little by little" and you plead, moreover, that only the
hands of fallen enemies are cut off, and that if hands are cut
off "enemies" not quite dead, and who, after recovery, have
have had the bad taste to
come to the missionaries and
show them their stumps, it
was due to an original mistake in thinking that they
were dead. *From Debate in
Belgian Parliament, July, 1903.*

SUPPLEMENTARY
Written for the 1906 edition by
MARK TWAIN

Since the first edition of this pamphlet was issued, the Congo story has entered upon a new chapter. The king's Commission concedes the correctness of the delineation contained in the foregoing pages. It affirms the prevalence of frightful abuses under the king's rule. For eight months the king held back the Report, but his commissioners had been too deeply moved by the horrors unfolded before them in their visit to the Congo State and the testimony presented to them had reached the world through other sources. The digest of the report, as forwarded from Brussels to the European and American press, was skillfully edited; and the report itself does its best to gloss over the king's responsibility for the shame; but the story told in the genuine document is essentially as hideous as anything found in the depositions of plain-speaking missionaries. So the facts are clear—indisputable, undisputed. The train of revilers of missionary testimony, whose roseate pictures of conditions under the king's rule have beguiled the uninformed, hurries out at the wings and Leopold is left to hold the stage, with the skeleton that refuses longer to stay hidden in his Congo closet.

One thing the report omits to do. It does not brand or judge the system out of which the foul breed of iniquities has sprung—the king's claim to personal ownership of 800,000 square miles of territory, with all their products, and his employment of savage hordes to realize on his claim.

Judgment of this policy the Commission holds to be beyond its function. Being thus disqualified for striking at the roots of the enormity, the commissioners propose such superficial reforms as occur to them. And the king hastens to take up with their suggestion by calling to his assistance in the work of reform a new Commission. Of this body of fourteen members all but two are committed by their past record to defense and maintenance of the king's Congo policy.

So ends the king's investigation of himself; doubtless less jubilantly than he had planned, but withal as ineffectively as it was foredoomed to end. One stage is achieved. The next in order is action by the Powers responsible for the existence of the Congo State. The United States is one of these. Such procedure is advocated in petitions to the President and Congress, signed by John Wanamaker, Lyman Abbott, Henry Van Dyke, David Starr Jordan and many other leading citizens. If ever the sisterhood of civilized nations have just occasion to go up to The Hague or some other accessible meeting place, a foreordained hour for their assembling has now struck.

SOME THINGS THE REPORT OF THE KING'S COMMISSION SAYS

"Apart from the rough plantations which barely suffice to feed the natives themselves and to supply the stations, all the fruits of the soil are considered as the property of the State or of the concessionaire societies....It has even been admitted that on the land occupied by them the natives cannot dispose of the produce of the soil except to the extent in which they did so before the constitution of the State."

"Each official in charge of a Station, or agent in charge of a factory, claimed from the natives, without asking himself on what grounds, the most divers imposts in labor or in kind, either to satisfy his own needs and those of his Station, or to exploit the riches of the Domain....The agents themselves regulated the tax and saw to its collection and had a direct interest in increasing its amount, since they received proportional bonuses on the produce thus collected."

"Missionaries, both Catholic and Protestant, whom we heard at Leopoldville, were unanimous in accentuating the general wretchedness existing in the region. One of them said that "this system which compels the natives to feed 3,000 workmen at Leopoldville will, if continued for another five years, wipe out the population of the district."

"Judicial officials have informed us of the sorry consequences of the porterage system; it exhausts the unfortunate people subjected to it, and threatens them with partial destruction."

"In the majority of cases the native must go one or two days' march every fortnight, until he arrives at that part of the forest where the rubber vines can be met with in a certain degree of abundance. There the collector passes a number of days in a miserable existence. He has to build himself an improvised shelter which cannot, obviously, replace his hut. He has not the food to which he is accustomed. He is deprived of his wife, exposed to the inclemencies of the weather and the attacks of wild beasts. When once he has collected the rubber he must bring it to the State station, or to that of the Company, and only then can he return to his village where he can sojourn for barely more than two or three days because the next demand is upon him."

"It was barely denied that in the various posts of the A.B.I.R. which we visited, the imprisonment of women hostages, the subjection of the chiefs to servile labor, the humiliations meted out to them, the flogging of rubber collectors, the brutality of the black employees set over the prisoners, were the rule commonly followed."

"According to the witnesses, these auxiliaries, especially those stationed in the villages, convert themselves into despots, claiming the women and the food; they kill without pity all those who attempt to resist their whims. The truth of the charges is borne out by a mass of evidence and official reports."

"The consequences are often very murderous. And one must not be astonished. If in the course of these delicate operations, whose object it is to seize hostages and to intimidate the natives, constant watch cannot be exercised over the sanguinary instincts of the soldiers, when orders to punish are given by superior authority, it is difficult to prevent the expedition from degenerating into massacres, accompanied by pillage and incendiarism."

THE UNITED STATES GOVERNMENT AND THE CONGO STATE

The International Association of the Congo was recognized by the United States April 22, 1884. Nine months afterward, recognition was secured from Germany and, later, successively from the other European Powers. Two international conferences were held at which the Powers constituted themselves guardians of the people of the Congo territory, the Association binding itself to regard the principles of administration adopted. In both these conferences the United States government prominently participated. The Act of Berlin was not submitted by the President of the United States for ratification by the Senate because its adoption as a whole was thought by him to involve responsibility for support of the territorial claims of rival Powers in the Congo region. The Act of Brussels, with a proviso safeguarding this point, was formally ratified by the United States. Whether we are without obligation to reach a hand to this expiring people, the intelligent reader will judge for himself.

> Stanley saw neither fortress nor flag of any civilization save that of the United States, which he carried along the arterial water course....The first appeal for recognition and for moral support was naturally and justly made to the government whose flag was first carried across the region.
> —*Mr. Kasson in North American Review, February, 1SS6.*

This Government at the outset testified its lively interest in the well-being and future progress of the vast region now committed to your

Majesty's wise care, by being the first among the Powers to recognize the flag of the International Association of the Congo as that of a friendly State."

—*President Cleveland to King Leopold, September 11, 1885.*

The recognition by the United States was the birth into new life of the Association, seriously menaced as its existence was by opposing interests and ambitions.

— *Mr. Stanley, The Congo, vol. I, page 383.*

He (the President of the United States) desires to see in the delimitation of the region which shall be subjected to this beneficent rule (of the International Association of the Congo) the widest expansion consistent with the just territorial rights of other governments.

—*Address of Mr. Kasson, U. S. Representative at Berlin Conference, 1S84.*

So marked was the acceptance by the Berlin Conference of the views presented on the part of the United States that Herr von Bunsen, reviewing the action of the Conference, assigns after Germany the first place of influence in the Conference to the United States.

—*Mr. Kasson in North American Review, February, 1886.*

In sending a representative to this Assembly, the Government of the U. S. has wished to show the great interest and deep sympathy it feels in the great work of philanthropy which the Conference seeks to realize. Our country must feel beyond all others an immense interest in the work of this Assembly.

—*Mr. Terrell, U. S. Representative at Brussels Conference, 1st session, November 19, 1889.*

Mr. Terrell informs the Conference that he has been authorized by this Government to sign the General Act adopted by the Conference.

The President says that the U. S. Minister's communication will be received by the Conference with extreme satisfaction.

—*Records of Brussels Conference, June 28, 1890.*

Claiming, as at Berlin, to speak in the name of Almighty God, the signatories (at Brussels) declared themselves to be "equally animated by the firm intention of putting an end to the crimes and devastations engendered by the traffic in African slaves, of protecting effectually the aboriginal populations and of ensuring the benefits of peace and civilization."

—*Civilization in Congoland, H. R. Fox Bourne.*

The President continues to hope that the Government of the U. S., which was the first to recognize the Congo Free State, will not be one of the last to give it the assistance of which it may stand in need.

—*Remarks of Belgian President of Brussels Conference, session May 14 1890.*

A WITNESS BEFORE
THE COMMISSION:
REV. JOHN H. HARRIS,
MISSIONARY AT
BARINGA, CONGO STATE

A WITNESS BEFORE
THE COMMISSION:
LOMBOTO,
A NATIVE OF BARINGA,
CONGO STATE

"There, great chiefs from Europe, stands the man who murdered our fathers, mothers, brothers and sisters for rubber. Why, why I say, has he done this?" —*The witness Lomboto, confronting the Director of the A.B.I.R. Society at the hearing at Baringa.*

OUGHT KING LEOPOLD TO BE HANGED?*

Interview by Mr. W. T. Stead with the Rev. John H. Harris, Baringa, Congo State, in the *English Review of Reviews* for September 1901.

For the somewhat startling suggestion in the heading of this interview, the missionary interviewed is in no way responsible. The credit of it, or, if you like, the discredit, belongs entirely to the editor of the *Review,* who, without dogmatism, wishes to pose the question as a matter for serious discussion. Since Charles I's head was cut off, opposite Whitehall, nearly two hundred and fifty years ago, the sanctity which doth hedge about a king has been held in slight and scant regard by the Puritans and their descendants. Hence there is nothing antecedently shocking or outrageous in the discussion of the question whether the acts of any Sovereign are such as to justify the calling in of the services of the public executioner. It is not, of course, for a journalist to pronounce judgment, but no function of the public writer is *so* imperative as that of calling attention to great wrongs, and no duty is more imperious than that of insisting that no rank or station should be allowed to shield from justice the real criminal when he is once discovered.

The controversy between the Congo Reform Association and the Emperor of the Congo has now arrived at a stage in which it is necessary

---

* The above article which came to hand as the foregoing was in press is commended to the king and to readers of his Soliloquy. — M. T.

to take a further step towards the redress of unspeakable wrongs and the punishment of no less
unspeakable criminals. The Rev. J. H. Harris, an
English missionary, has lived for the last seven
years in that region of Central Africa—the Upper
Congo—which King Leopold has made over to
one of his vampire groups of financial associates
(known as the A.B.I.R. Society) on the strictly business basis of a half share in the profits wrung from
the blood and misery of the natives. He has now
returned to England, and last month he called
at Mowbray House to tell me the latest from the
Congo. Mr. Harris is a young man in a dangerous
state of volcanic fury, and no wonder. After living
for seven years face to face with the devastations
of the vampire State, it is impossible to deny that
he does well to be angry. When he began, as is the
wont of those who have emerged from the depths,
to detail horrifying stories of murder, the outrage
and torture of women, the mutilation of children,
and the whole infernal category of horrors, served
up with the background of cannibalism, sometimes voluntary and sometimes, incredible though
it seems, enforced by the orders of the officers, I
cut him short, and said:

"Dear Mr. Harris, as in Oriental despatches the
India Office translator abbreviates the first page of
the letter into two words 'after compliments,' or
'a. c.,' so let us abbreviate our conversation about
the Congo by the two words 'after atrocities,' or 'a.
a.' They are so invariable and so monotonous, as
Lord Percy remarked in the House the other day,
that it is unnecessary to insist upon them. There is
no longer any dispute in the mind of any reason-
able person as to what is going on in the Congo. It
is the economical exploitation of half a continent

carried on by the use of armed force wielded by officials the aim-all and be-all of whose existence is to extort the maximum amount of rubber in the shortest possible time in order to pay the largest possible dividend to the holders of shares in the concessions."

"Well," said Mr. Harris reluctantly, for he is so accustomed to speaking to persons who require to be told the whole dismal tale from A to Z, "what is it you want to know?"

"I want to know," I said, "whether you consider the time is ripe for summoning King Leopold before the bar of an international tribunal to answer for the crimes perpetrated under his orders and in his interest in the Congo State."

Mr. Harris paused for a moment, and then said:—"That depends upon the action which the king takes upon the report of the Commission, which is now in his hands."

"Is that report published?"

"No," said Mr. Harris. "And it is a question whether it will ever be published. Greatly to our surprise, the Commission, which every one expected would be a mere blind whose appointment was intended to throw dust in the eyes of the public, turned out to be composed of highly respectable persons who heard the evidence most impartially, refused no *bona fide* testimony produced by trustworthy witnesses, and were overwhelmed by the multitudinous horrors brought before them, and who, we feel, *must* have arrived at conclusions which necessitate an entire revolution in the administration of the Congo."

"Are you quite sure, Mr. Harris, that this is so?"

"Yes," said Mr. Harris, "quite sure. The Commission impressed us all in the Congo very favorably. Some of its members seemed to us admirable specimens of public-spirited, independent statesmen. They realized that they were acting in judicial capacity; they knew that the eyes of Europe were upon them, and, instead of making their inquiry a farce, they made it a reality, and their conclusions must be, I feel sure, so damning to the State, that if King Leopold were to take no action but to allow the whole infernal business to proceed unchecked, any international tribunal which had powers of a criminal court, would upon the evidence of the Commission alone, send those responsible to the gallows."

"Unfortunately," I said, "at present The Hague Tribunal is not armed with the powers of an international assize court, nor is it qualified to place offenders, crowned or otherwise, in the dock. But don't you think that in the evolution of society the constitution of such a criminal court is a necessity?"

"It would be a great convenience at present," said Mr. Harris; "nor would you need one atom of evidence beyond the report of the Commission to justify the hanging of whoever is responsible for the existence and continuance of such abominations."

"Has anybody seen the text of the report?" I asked.

"As the Commission returned to Brussels in March, some of the contents of that report are an open secret. A great deal of the evidence has been published by the Congo Reform Association. In the Congo the Commissioners admitted two things: first, that the evidence was overwhelming as to the existence of the evils which had hitherto been denied, and secondly, that they vindicated the character of the missionaries. They discovered, as anyone will who goes to that country, that it is the missionaries, and the missionaries alone, who constitute the permanent European element. The Congo State officials come out ignorant of the language, knowing nothing of the country, and with no other sense of their duties beyond that of supporting the concession companies in extorting rubber. They are like men who are dumb and deaf and blind, nor do they wish to be otherwise. In two or three years they vanish, giving place to other migrants as ignorant as themselves, whereas the missionaries remain on the spot year after year; they are in personal touch with the people, whose language they speak, whose customs they respect, and whose lives they endeavor to defend to the best of their ability."

"But, Mr. Harris," I remarked, "was there not a certain Mr. Grenfell, a Baptist Missionary, who has been all these years a convinced upholder of the Congo State?"

"'Twas true," said Mr. Harris, "and pity 'tis 'twas true; but 'tis no longer true. Mr. Grenfell has had his eyes opened at last, and he has now taken his place among those who are convinced. He could no longer resist the overwhelming evidence that has been brought against the Congo Administration."*

"Was the nature of the Commissioners' report," I resumed, "made known to the officials of the State before they left the Congo?"

"To the head officials—yes," said Mr. Harris.

"With what result?"

"In the case of the highest official in the Congo, the man who corresponds in Africa to

---

* Mr. Grenfell's station is in the Lower Congo, a section remote from the vast rubber areas of the interior.

Lord Curzon in India, no sooner was he placed in possession of the conclusions of the Commission than the appalling significance of their indictment convinced him that the game was up, and he went into his room and cut his throat.

"I was amazed upon returning to Europe to find how little the significance of this suicide was appreciated. A paragraph in the newspaper announced the suicide of a Congo official. None of those who read that paragraph could realize the fact that that suicide had the same significance to the Congo that the suicide, let us say, of Lord Milner would have had if it had taken place immediately on receiving the conclusions of a Royal Commission sent out to report upon his administration in South Africa."

"Well, if that be so, Mr. Harris," I said, "and the Governor-General cuts his throat rather than face the ordeal and disgrace of the exposure, I am almost beginning to hope that we may see King Leopold in the dock at The Hague, after all."

"I will comment upon that," Mr. Harris said, "by quoting you Mrs. Sheldon's remark made before myself and my colleagues, Messrs. Bond, Ellery, Ruskin, Walbaum and Whiteside, on May 19th last year, when, in answer to our question, 'Why should King Leopold be afraid of submitting his case to The Hague tribunal?' Mrs. Sheldon answered, 'Men do not go to the gallows and put their heads in a noose if they can avoid it.'"

Contributors

Samuel Clemens, best known by his pen name Mark Twain, was born in 1835 and grew up in Hannibal, Missouri. The author of some of the most beloved works in American literature, including the novels *The Adventures of Tom Sawyer* and *Adventures of Huckleberry Finn*, Twain worked as a typesetter, a riverboat pilot, and a miner before starting his career as a journalist and writer. Twain's sharp wit and keen insights earned him a legacy as one of the country's greatest humorists. Mark Twain died in 1910 at age seventy-four.

Hunt Hawkins is Professor and Chair of the English Department at the University of South Florida. He has published extensively on Mark Twain as well as Joseph Conrad, E. M. Forster, James Joyce, Chinua Achebe, and Aime Cesaire on topics involving imperialism, particularly in the Congo. Previously he has taught at Kurasini College in Tanzania, Texas Southern University, Stanford, University of Minnesota, and Florida State University. He has also served as President of the South Atlantic Modern Language Association.